VANISHED

ISBN: 979-8-218-09616-8

Contents

DEDICATION

To my mom, who never gave up on me and always believed in me with endless patience and love.

To my amazing fiancé, who has encouraged and motivated me, helping me believe in myself in the darkest times.

To my dad… the one who isn't blood but stepped up and never turned his back on me, who taught me to be tough, to grow through to my future.

How far would you go
to save someone you love?

<u>ONE</u>

Pancakes sizzle on the stovetop in front of me. It's almost time to leave for our flight to Daytona, Florida. The pitter-patter of my heart grows faster as we get closer to our long-awaited vacation.

The warm, sweet bread-like smell of breakfast calms my mind. This will be a special week. I can't wait to see Alison's face light up like a kid on Christmas morning when she sees the ocean for the first time. Ten years ago, when we got married, we had little money. But I knew one day, we would have our dream honeymoon and now it's right around the corner.

"I hate that money made it hard to have a vacation like this," I say, pulling open the drawer and taking out a fork.

"But it paid off, don't you think?" Alison nudges my arm with her elbow before walking upstairs.

"Yes, it sure has."

We both have busy schedules. Alison's not home until seven at night, and when I'm home, I'm doing paperwork for clients. Real estate can be time-consuming, and so can her job as a veterinarian assistant.

"Jason! Do you have the notebook?" Alison calls out from upstairs. I can hear her rummaging through her nightstand.

"Yes, babe!"

A notebook of fun things to do.

Alison is an organized person who wants to ensure we have our entire trip planned ahead of time. I am a go-with-the-flow kind of guy, but I try my best to plan something for us, and I can guarantee she will love this trip. This notebook has restaurants we will eat at and gift shops where we'll ogle at fancy items to put on our mantle. There are also other date ideas she has in mind for us.

I set the pancakes on our plates, drizzle maple syrup over the top, sit at the table, and dig into mine.

"Calm down, honey. Chew for once." Her giggles grow closer as she walks down the stairs.

"Well, hurry. We are going to be late."

"Hey now," she scoffs, "I have to make sure I am comfortable on the flight."

I roll my eyes and smile. Alison is something else.

The amount of love I have for this woman is hard to describe.

We've been through many struggles, like choosing between milk and bread, even after borrowing money from family and friends to get by. We rarely missed paying bills on time, but even once was too late for our liking. Through all the chaos and struggle, we've managed to gain control of our debt.

For the last three years, we have been living within our means and have been saving every dime for our honeymoon.

Each time we had to dip into our savings to catch up on a bill, it was done with a scowl, knowing what we were taking from, but it helped us out in the long run.

Every day when I see Alison, it feels like I've been slapped in the face by emotions that create goosebumps throughout my body. When she walks through the front door or shows that flawless dimpled smile, I feel like a teenager again.

The flight to Florida wasn't as scary as I'd thought. Time flew by, thanks to the classical music blaring through my earbuds. Good thing, too. Whenever I worry, my body wants to drop through the floor. Being this high up isn't my cup of tea, but Alison loves it and that's all that matters. She's all that matters.

Less than an hour later, we arrive at the Hard Rock Hotel, which sits right on the beach. Alison has never been close to any coast before this vacation, and this state is beautiful during the summer months.

As a kid, I lived in Long Beach, California, until I was eight. My parents moved the three of us away to Missouri after getting new jobs. I begged them to stay, but when they moved us anyway, I didn't speak to them for three whole days. I didn't want to leave my friends or start over in a new school, and I didn't want to go to one of those boring states that didn't even have an ocean nearby. The ocean is the place my uncle took me to as a kid all the time before he passed away. I didn't want to leave. We were so close it felt like I was leaving him and the memories behind. But if we had never moved, I would've never met Alison.

"How did you earn detention?" Alison asks, pushing her hair behind her right ear.

"Silly prank against the teacher." I couldn't help but laugh a little.

"Oh yeah? What kind of prank?" She stops walking and looks at me as she clutches textbooks against her chest.

"Bubble wrapped his car because I got an F on my history paper."

"Of course," she says with a small laugh, rolling her eyes and giving a small smile.

"Oh my god, the hotel is beautiful!" Alison says, opening the door of the taxi and ending my memory.

"It sure is."

I lift our luggage from the trunk, then walk to the driver's side. I pay the driver and take my wife's hand as we head toward the extravagant building. Palm trees stand high and sway with the wind.

I open the glass doors. "My lady," I say with a smirk.

Alison smiles and walks inside.

My hand sweats under the handles of the luggage as it rolls across the floor. We head to the front desk, where a man greets us and gives us our room keys. Our room is on the seventh floor. Thank God for the invention of elevators.

The hotel room has a queen-size bed with a white and gray striped bedspread, fluffy white pillows, and a white carpet that feels plush under my feet. Black picture frames with music notes hang on the wall above the bed.

"Oh, wow! Oh, wow!" Alison squeals.

She opens the glass doors to the balcony and steps outside. Sheer gray curtains hang from rods set on the balcony above us, giving us additional privacy. She throws them aside to expand our view of the coast.

"Damn, maybe we need to move here!" I say before I drop our suitcases by the bed and join her on the balcony. I can see the ocean from the front door, but standing on the terrace makes my heart race, especially when my beautiful wife is standing on it, making the ocean view even more amazing.

"Maybe!"

The sun glistens on the waves like a sparkling diamond. I wrap my arms around her waist, kiss her on the cheek, and whisper, "I love you."

She turns and kisses my lips. "I love you too."

"Come on, let me show you something." I take her hand and head toward the bathroom. "No peeking."

She puts a hand over her eyes and giggles.

I smile, opening the bathroom door. "Okay, you can look."

She uncovers her eyes and gasps, "Oh, Jason!"

Her eyes open wide, and a smile flickers across her face like a hologram. Her dimples are flawless, with two adorable dots that mirror her smile lines.

Alison steps into the bathroom. On the sink are two vases of roses, and small candles light up the entire room in every area they can sit on, while soft white towels lie on a rack next to the tub. She will love wrapping up in one after a warm relaxing bath.

The room smells of apples, one of her favorite scents.

"You like it?" I ask. I called the hotel two days before so it could be set up in time to surprise her.

She looks over at me, her ocean-blue eyes filling with tears. "I love it!" Alison kisses my cheek and begins undressing for her bath.

"Okay, I'll be back soon."

"Wait. Where are you going?" she asks, while pulling her hair up in a ponytail.

"I'm getting the boat ready for our dinner date tonight."

"You're taking me out on a boat?" She flashes her beautiful smile as joy fills her bright eyes.

I walk back toward her and help her into the warm bath. "Yes, now relax. I'll text you when to come down."

She nods, and I kiss her forehead before heading out of the hotel room.

The sun is setting, perfect for the start of our date night. The ocean water feels warm on my feet. This means Alison will be comfortable.

Our runabout boat is ready for us. It's been my favorite style since I was a kid. My great-uncle had one of these at his lake house.

The exterior is brown, with white seating and flooring. The strawberry wine I ordered sits on the seat, waiting to be guzzled down.

After a while, I take my phone out of my pocket and text Alison, telling her to come outside. My hands become sweaty as I wait. I want tonight to be perfect. I shove my phone back into my pocket, grab the bouquet of roses from the boat seat, and hold them close to my chest.

"Jason?" a soft voice calls out.

I turn around and smile.

Alison walks down the dock, her little white sandals slapping against her feet. She's wearing a white floral cover up over her bright blue bikini.

The fine lines around her eyes make me think of all the laughter we've shared over the past ten years. She's put up with me all this time. God, she deserves this vacation.

"Do you like it?"

"You wanted to impress me, huh?" she laughs.

"You deserve this, baby." I hand her the roses.

Her cheeks tint red when she grabs the flowers and looks at me one more time before stepping onto the boat. I follow. I love seeing her happy.

The night has been going well. We've had a few drinks and strawberry chocolate desserts and have been cracking funny jokes and recalling moments.

"Today is our first day of fun on this honeymoon."

She looks at me and smiles. "And?"

"Ready to leave yet?" I smirk.

She throws her head back. "Heck no! I want to stay here forever!"

I kiss her on the cheek and look out at the ocean.

The light from the boat makes it easy to see out in front of us, and the ocean's waves are a relaxing sight. I bend down to grab something beneath my seat.

"What are you doing?"

"Grabbing your gift."

"Okay," she says.

I pick up the small red rectangle box and smile, clutching it in the palm of my left hand before looking back at her.

But she's not in her seat.

Confused, I stare at where Alison was sitting just a moment before. Her clothes are lying in her seat. I grab her white coverup and inspect it.

"What the heck…" I whisper to myself. I place the coverup back down. My head feels foggy, and I look back out into the ocean. I stand up, lean over, and begin frantically looking around the sides of the boat, swishing my arms in the water, and hoping to feel for her. Did she fall in? I didn't hear a splash… It's dark, and the light only goes so far out. I move the light around the boat, but there are no signs of her.

Am I hallucinating?

"*Alison!*" I scream before falling back into my seat.

I close my eyes and take a deep breath.

She's vanished.

Amy Rose

TWO

Our boat is not too far out. I barely get to shore before jumping off and sprinting for the hotel lobby. Half-blinded by panic, I spot the man who gave us our keys standing behind the counter. I pat around for my phone and take it out of my pocket, only to see the screen wouldn't come to life. Of course, it's dead.

He looks up from his paperwork as I sprint to him. My breath is nearly gone, and my throat feels incredibly dry from running.

"Sir! Please help!"

"Are you okay?" he asks, his brows furrowing.

"My wife, she's missing!" I gasp, trying to catch my breath.

With a concerned look, he walks around the desk, throws an arm over my shoulder, and escorts me to an office area.

Good thing he took me out of the busy lobby, because as I see the chair, all I can do is collapse into it with my face in my hands and elbows resting on my knees. My entire body feels numb, and my heart is pounding with each breath.

"What's your name?"

"Jason," I say as I rub the back of my neck.

"My name is Jamie. I'll call the police." He picks up his desk phone, dials it, and explains my situation. He takes a glance at me and thanks them.

"Jason, they'll be here in ten minutes," he says while walking over to a white mini fridge. "Water?" he holds a bottle out to me.

I nod and take it from his hands, open it up, and gulp it down like it's the last drink on earth.

My head feels like it's going to explode with everything going on. Where is Alison? Did she fall overboard? No… I would've heard it… Her clothes were lying there as if no one wore them yet. The date was going great until she vanished in the middle of the ocean… into thin air like dust in the wind. Poof. Gone.

Lost in my racing thoughts, I almost didn't see the police officer enter several minutes later. A tall man with dark brown hair approaches me.

"Jason, my name is Officer Kevin Dawson." He flips open a notepad and takes out a pen from the spiral spine, then sits on the edge of the desk. "Can you explain what happened?"

I look up, and I don't see Jamie in sight. I am too far into my thoughts to notice when he left.

"I don't know how to explain it," I say.

"She's missing, correct?" he asks.

"Yes, we're on our honeymoon right now… we were on the boat and the next thing I know, she's gone, poof. Like she didn't exist." I lean back into the chair and look at him.

"Did she fall in?" the officer asks while writing notes.

"I figured she did, and I just didn't hear it. Can we get a rescue team out there?" I ask and stand up from the chair.

His face drops. He looks at me as if his soul has left his body. No sign of emotion is on any part of his wrinkled, pale face.

"What's wrong?" I ask.

"Nothing. I've got everything I need. You are free to go." He grabs his notebook from the desk and stands.

"That's it?" I clench my fists.

"That's all we need." He walks toward the door.

"Can I at least file a police report?" I'm raising my voice now, but I can't seem to control the volume.

"She's an adult. People run from their own lives every day." He opens the door, gesturing for me to leave.

"Are you insane?" Even though I had downed a bottle of water, my voice cracks. I can feel the blood rushing to my face. "File a report, or I'm suing you and your entire police department!"

"There's nothing I can do right now."

"What the fuck ever! I'll see your ass in court." I slap my hand against the door and walk toward the elevator. Before the doors close, I stare at the officer. He side-eyes me while facing Jamie. Something is odd.

Opening the hotel room, I quickly place my phone on the charger and grab the hotel room phone, dialing my brother.

"Hello?" His deep voice echoes through the phone.

"Hey Alex, it's Jason. Something bad has happened," I say and sit on the chair next to the phone.

"What's going on?" he asks.

"Alison is missing."

When I explain the situation to him, there is a moment of silence.

"Maybe you should come home. We can figure this out here," he suggests.

I shake my head. "No, I think I need to stay and look for her myself before I proceed any further."

"Okay, just call me when you arrive home."

I hang the phone up and lean back in the chair.

Something was wrong, and it feels like someone was trying to cover it up.

waited at the hotel for two days after the incident, combing the beach myself and I tried calling and speaking to the officer who came out to the hotel, but he has been unavailable. There is no sign of Alison. Alex, being a private investigator, might help me figure this.

It's as if she never existed.

Not knowing what else to do, I board a plane home. I didn't want to leave Florida knowing my wife vanished here, but the officer won't help, and I don't know anyone here who will.

I feel useless.

The plane finally touches down, and I look around my surroundings. Everyone on the plane is grabbing their belongings while I sit there and look out this small, circular window. I can't help but wonder if coming home so soon was a mistake. And all I can think is 'Alex will help'.

Back home, I hear the doorknob jiggle. "Come in!" I holler from the couch.

The door opens, and there is Alex.

"Hug me, brother!" he hollers.

Alex is five years older than me, but goofier than I am.

I stand there and stare at him, no smile or frown on my face, just a blank stare.

"Oh, come here!" He pulls me into his arms, and I tear up.

"Look, man, we'll find Alison." He pushes past me and drops his suitcase on the couch. "But we can't do this right until you get yourself together."

Alex sniffs the air and his nose scrunches up. "Go shower. You look and smell awful."

Wordlessly, I turn and walk upstairs. It's only been two days since I got home, but the trash and dishes have already piled up. I haven't bothered to shower or change my clothes. It does stink in here. I guess I haven't bothered to notice.

Before I shower, I pass through our bedroom, a place I've been avoiding since I got back. Alison's favorite body mist sits on the dresser in a little pink bottle, ready for her to walk past and grab. As a joke, I bought her ten at once for her birthday last spring.

"You'll never have to buy them again," I teased her.

She always sprays the mist away from her neck once, then spins through it, dispersing the aroma throughout the room and across her clothes.

Alison even sprays the entire house once a day with it. I love that about her.

I hold the bottle up to my nose and breathe in. Tears brim my eyes. I spray the vanilla-scented mist on my neck before placing the container back down with a sigh.

Reluctantly, I head into the bathroom for my shower.

Hot water streams down my tense muscles. The usual ways I take care of myself seem impossible to do now. They make me feel selfish, when I don't know what happened to her or where she is.

I used to love hot showers. I used to blast the heat until the steam fogged up the mirror and spilled into our bedroom like a sauna. But… it's different this time.

Alison made fun of me for loving showers like that. She even asked if I was secretly a rainforest creature or something silly.

The water feels like nothing now, without her here, without knowing what happened to her. It could be ice cold, and I'd feel the same.

When I return downstairs, I see Alex sitting at the kitchen table, looking down at his computer.

"Jason, did the officer ever tell you why he wouldn't investigate further?

"No, and he acted strange." I shrug my shoulders.

"Strange how?"

"His tone went from worried to slightly annoyed."

Alex fidgets with his thumbs. "Okay, you turned around, and she was just gone?"

I nod and sit in the chair across from him, slamming my fist on the table. The echoing *pow* doesn't feel as satisfying as I was hoping.

"How does someone vanish like that?" I ask.

Alex places his chin on the palm of his hand. "I don't know, but I find it odd that the police didn't do much. It's out of character for them." The clock shows midnight, and I'm trying to fall asleep. Alex is on the couch downstairs. I'm thankful to have a brother who can help me out, but I don't understand why the police won't. I should have stayed in Florida and drilled the police even more to help me find her, but now that I think about it, why does it feel like the police are involved? How do you accuse an officer without being sent to jail?

Memories of Alison have been inserting themselves non-stop, and they're clear as day. I remember the time she wanted a tattoo of a cross underneath her right ear.

"A plain cross?" I ask.

"No, I want vines wrapping around it." Her creative self is at it again.

"Alright, no crying, though, if you're going for something more painful."

She smacks my arm and laughs. "Shut up!"

When I mimic her laugh, she slaps my arm again and laughs harder.

"You're going to make me pee myself!" Tears form in her eyes from her hysterical laughter fit.

We almost couldn't breathe. Eventually, we run out of air and collapse into a cuddle, her vanilla-scented hair strewn on my face.

I pull her closer and kiss her head, then her lips. "I love you, Alison."

I close my eyes and soon fall asleep.

Amy Rose

THREE

When I wake up, my head is pounding, and my mouth is so dry my tongue feels like a hunk of lead. I spread out my left arm to Alison's side of the bed. I see her for an instant; all tucked in, covers drawn up around her delicate chin, that wild blonde hair pulled into a messy bun. But it's not real. My head is still foggy and slow as I make my way downstairs. My life feels sluggish. Nothing feels real anymore.

The main floor of the house smells of bacon, and my stomach growls. I haven't eaten since yesterday morning.

"Hey, bro!" Alex hollers from the kitchen.

I walk in there to see him cooking in dark blue pajama bottoms decorated with gold stars.

"You're a private investigator. You shouldn't dress like that." I can't help but laugh at him.

"Look, just because I'm a fancy man doesn't mean I dress like one at home." He sets our plates on the kitchen table with cheese-filled omelets and bacon on the side. There is already a pitcher of orange juice in the middle and two glasses. He grabs a small bag of potato chips and places them on his plate.

I stare.

"What?" he asks.

"I've never seen you cook. Like, not once in our whole lives."

Alex laughs and shrugs his shoulders. "Well, being married for a few years, you learn to do things."

"How is Marissa? Is she okay with this arrangement?"

"She doesn't like us being apart too long, but we'll be fine."

I nod and sit at the kitchen table.

"Jason, we need to talk." Alex sits down across from me.

"What's going on, Alex?" I glance at his fingers; he is fumbling his thumbs together. Why does he sound so nervous?

"We need to make a plan." He ruffles through his green and blue bookbag and pulls out a yellow notepad.

"We both know Alison vanishing the way she did makes no sense," he says.

"Right, so what do we need to do?"

"Well. For starters, we need to keep this between us until we figure out how and why." He writes notes on the pad. "We can't have people asking questions."

"Why not?"

"Well, we don't need the media at the front door."

"Okay… but don't we want that?"

"No, because," he flicks his thumb up, "One, you left Florida before trying to track her down, which will make people create assumptions about you." He extends his index finger. "And two, she vanished oddly. We don't need conspiracy theorists at your front door."

"Hey, YOU told me to leave. I wanted to stay!"

"I know, but it still doesn't look great, and you need to go back to your normal routine, at least try to be in the right mindset for Alison," he says.

"I can't pretend like everything is fine,"

"I'm not saying to, but you need to go out and run or something before you go nuts."

"Maybe I don't want to. My wife is fucking missing. Don't you think it's best I just stay and figure out where she is?" I stand up from the chair.

"No, you need to be sane for her."

I roll my eyes and walk out the front door, leaving my untouched food.

I usually jog around the block five times every morning to start my day. Alex has convinced me to keep going, so I am not stuck inside the house moping around. He says it's not suitable for my mental state in this situation. He's right, as always.

Instead of jogging, I take my bike out and ride. Alison bought the dark blue Roadmaster for my birthday last year. Twice a week, we go riding.

Our neighborhood is filled with beautiful brick homes. Every sidewalk has children's chalk games and drawings. Alison and I have ten years of history here.

On our weekly summer walks, I shake tree branches and watch Alison run and scream to avoid the sudden clouds of beetles. She *hates* bugs.

I set my bike against the telephone pole and enter the gas station a few blocks from home.

"Hey, Jason! How are you?" the associate greets me.

"Hey, Derek, I'm good. Grabbing some snacks."

I walk toward the freezer doors, look over what I want to buy, and take root beer, Bud Light, and chips.

Alison and I come here once a week to grab snacks, alcohol, and soda for movie nights or games we have planned. A little tradition we have together.

"How's Alison?" he asks.

"Good," I lie straight through my teeth.

I place my items on the counter, he scans them, and I pay with cash before returning to my bike, hanging the bag onto the right handlebar.

Lying about Alison breaks my heart. Alison wouldn't like that I'm drinking and eating during my problems.

I arrive home to see Alex sitting on the front porch swing, staring at his laptop with his brows furrowed and his chin resting on the palm of his hand.

I drop my bike by the tree and set the snacks and drinks on the porch. My cell phone vibrates in my pocket. I take it out and see that Alison's boss is calling. *Shit.*

"Hello?"

"Hi, Jason, it's Maddie from the vet's office. Is Alison in? We haven't heard from her since you guys left, and she didn't come in today for her shift."

"Hi, Maddie. Thanks for checking in. She caught the flu the other day. She's still sick. I meant to call you for her yesterday..." And the lies continue.

"Oh, that poor girl, let her know Jessica will cover her shifts until she gets back. Tell her we hope she gets better soon."

"Will do," I say and hang up and walk toward Alex.

Alex looks up at me with his eyebrows lowered. He tips his computer toward me, and I realize he has an article open.

"MAN FROM FLORIDA MISSING IN THE STRANGEST WAY." the title reads.

"Now, a man with the name Jamie from the hotel you were staying at has vanished," he sighs. "Just like Alison did."

"Jamie? The receptionist?" I ask while sitting next to him on the swing.

"Yes. It says in this article he was a front desk receptionist at the Hard Rock Hotel. How did you know?"

"Do you have a photo?"

He scrolls down the page to a headshot.

My heart skips a beat. "He was the one who checked us in and also called the police when I ran in about Alison vanishing." I look at him. "But why didn't they report about Alison?"

"This is very weird, dude," he says, shrugging.

I nod.

First Alison and now Jamie, the receptionist?

I need to find answers. The world is making less sense to me.

I stand up and grab the bag of stuff I bought, reach for the front door, swing it open from frustration, and head to the kitchen to grab an ice-cold beer out of the fridge. I hear Alex's footsteps right behind me.

"Come on, man. Take a deep breath."

"Are you fucking kidding me?" I raise my voice. My hands are shaking with anger. "My wife is missing, and now the receptionist. In the SAME way."

I down the entire can of beer before throwing it into the trash.

I lean against the wall and take a deep breath. Alex tries to hug me, but I shift away from him.

"The gas station associate asked me how she was."

"What did you say?"

"I lied and told him she was fine."

I hate lying, especially when it involves my wife.

Amy Rose

<u>FOUR</u>

Alex has been trying to figure out what happened to Alison and Jamie. Every waking moment, he has his laptop open, a notepad in front of him, and newspapers printed out between timelines.

It has been stressing me out to the max. My body feels numb. Everything I do reminds me of Alison. When I touch the fridge, a drink, or even our bed, it feels like nothing is there… it's almost as if I've lost feeling.

I walk to the kitchen and make a bowl of cereal when my phone dings.

Jason, I am out running errands. I will be home in an hour.–Alex.

I finish my Frosted Flakes and place my bowl in the sink.

My phone dings again. I unlock the screen and see a notification from the "Weird News" community forum I'm a part of. **"Distress Call."** the title reads.

I click play. The video is slightly blurry, and the lighting is terrible. A woman with blonde hair appears on camera. She's wearing a white and blue hospital gown, and the room behind her looks like a science classroom.

"Help! My name is Alison Kendrick. I am being held in a facility. Someone, please help me!"

I inhale a sharp breath.

The video seems to have been filmed on a laptop camera. It gets cut short by Alison, closing it right after asking for help. But before she did, I could see her eyes move to the corner. Something must have spooked her.

My heart feels like it's been torn from my chest. I play it over twice to be sure I'm not hallucinating.

"Alison?" I breathe out.

I hear the front door unlock and run into the living room as Alex walks in with arms full of groceries.

"Woah, dude, you look like you have seen a ghost." Alex walks into the kitchen, which is connected to my living room, and sets the grocery bags on the table.

"What's wrong?" he asks.

"Alison."

He tilts his head. "What are you talking about?"

"Alison is alive!"

"What?" His eyes narrow.

I show him the forum on my cell phone.

He glances at me, the phone, and back at me without a word.

"What do we do? I can't just sit here!" I realize my heart is beating faster than it ever has.

"Save the video. We'll need it." Alex instructs.

I nod my head and press download on the screen.

Hours go by. Alex contacted the man who posted the report to ask him to take it down, and the man has yet to respond.

The minutes tick by far too slowly, but I'm still overwhelmed with relief that she's alive. I play the video repeatedly, just to hear her voice for the first time since she vanished. She sounds as if she is in a hurry. The shaking in her voice worries me.

I go outside and sit on the porch swing, and drown myself in thoughts of memories to keep my mind off what I had just found. It's getting dark, and I can hear Alex rummaging through the kitchen cooking dinner. I'm thinking that cooking is his coping mechanism during stressful times. My eyes wander to the rosebush near my privacy fence, and I smile, recalling the memory of me proposing to her.

"Alison, will you marry me?" I ask.

She gives a big smile as I kneel in front of her. I can see tears forming in her eyes.

"Oh, Jason, yes! A million times, yes!"

I slide the beautiful princess cut ring on her finger and stand back up, wrapping my arms around her, lifting her in the air, and spinning around with a kiss. It feels surreal, and I love every moment of this.

A memory I will never forget. I proposed to Alison in our backyard. She was so happy to see all the candles sitting around the picnic blanket with a laptop nearby, waiting to play our favorite but oldie movie, *Footloose*.

"Jason! Dinner is ready!"

Before going inside, I deeply inhale the fresh air to calm my nerves. I stand up and open the back door to step inside the house.

"Looks delicious, brother," I say while walking toward him to fill my plate up with the burgers and mac and cheese he made.

The smell is fantastic. My stomach growls, and I place a hand on my stomach.

"Someone's hungry," Alex says.

"Yeah, I haven't eaten much."

"No kidding."

He grabs his food, I grab mine, and we sit at the kitchen table.

Five minutes go by, and I have yet to touch my meal.

"Jason, eat." He points at my food.

I eat a few bites and move my plate to the middle of the table.

"Easier said than done, Alex."

"Jason, please."

"No! She has been missing longer than she should be! And nothing has been done to help find her!"

"This is not a normal missing person's case!" Alex yells.

"We can't just go to the public and ask for help!"

"Why? Why can't we?"

"If you want people at your doorstep assuming you did something or want people taking it to the media, go for it!"

Alex's phone buzzes. He grabs it from his back pocket and looks down at the screen.

"He responded—"

I snatch his phone from his hands to read what the guy says.

"Dude!" he scoffs.

"Shut up!"

Then I read the email aloud,

"Hello, Alex Kendrick. Thank you for your email. Somebody must have removed the post without my knowledge. I can't seem to find it. Something odd is going on, especially since I'm the only admin of the forum who can delete things. I received the video via email and shared the video on my forum, but have had a difficult time tracking it back to anyone. - Carson."

I check the forum to confirm, and luckily, I hadn't exited the app, so it's still there. I click play, but the video buffers. I try to reload the page, but the video vanishes. Just like her.

"Okay, that is weird." I put my hands behind my head and take a deep breath. "If he didn't take it down, then who did?"

"There has to be more to this. It's worrying me."

"That is what I'm afraid of."

"I think you should write in a journal."

I scrunch my nose. "Why?"

"It'll help with remembering timeframes, and you have a history of lashing out without talking to someone," he says.

"But she isn't dead. Why do I need to write how I feel?"

"Don't ask me questions, just trust me."

"We need to do something. We can't keep waiting. Something is off about this entire situation," I say.

"Look, I can only do so much. We could go to the police, yes, but I'm telling you right now, it's not the best idea." Alex finishes his food and puts his plate in the sink, then walks into the living room.

Why the fuck is he acting so weird? I think to myself.

The good news is that Alison is alive, but many unanswered questions exist. Confusion has clouded our minds, and we need to take action. But… how am I supposed to take action if I don't know where to start?

We can't tell the public, and we can't tell our family or the police. Alex is right, the last thing I need is the world coming at my family and me and throwing conspiracies around the situation.

Yes, the way she vanished is odd, and I know what kind of comments people would say. They would also try to pin her vanishing on me.

Alison's video makes me question where she could be. There was no physical kidnapping. Her entire being was gone in a flash, and her clothing was the only remainder of her. How is that even possible?

Alex had already gone to bed. But I can't sleep just yet.

I grab my phone from my nightstand drawer and sit in bed, leaning my back against my hardwood bedframe, and rewatch the video I downloaded earlier. Replaying this video is not a great idea for where my head is mentally, but there's got to be some clues.

Four numbers. I can barely make them out, but after experimenting with the video exposure and quality, I can see 1-0-1-0. It seems to be embedded in Alison's skin like a tattoo, the area around it red and irritated.

The room she is in has dimmed lights underneath cabinets behind her. There are no windows, and everything looks like she is sitting in a lab. I hurry out of my bedroom and down the stairs into the living room and shake Alex awake.

"Alex!" I yell, nudging his shoulder aggressively.

"What?" he says, rolling over and looking up at me.

"Alison has numbers on her!" I turn my phone around and show him.

He sits up and inspects my screen. He looks back at me with a frown. "What the hell?"

My eyes snap open, and my body's covered in a cold sweat. A scream erupts from my chest so hard my throat becomes sore. Paranoid, I look frantically around the room. The sun is out.

There are footsteps on the stairs and Alex comes into my room.

"What's wrong?" he asks.

"I'm fine." I push the covers off and place my feet on the floor. "Horrible dream."

"Sounded like more than a dream."

I ignore his remark and change the subject.

"What time is it?" I ask, rubbing my eyes.

"Two in the afternoon."

"Damn…"

"It's important you rest anyway," Alex says, walking toward the door.

<u>FIVE</u>

Dear… journal. Why does this sound weird? Alex says I should write about how I feel about plans and ideas… I don't know. We both fear the day we would go physically searching for her. Not knowing what to expect is terrifying, especially in a situation like this. Knowing what we know now about her vanishing shakes my soul in a way I never thought I could feel. My stomach feels hollow ever since I found out that she's alive, but something doesn't seem quite right. I don't understand how Alison could get to a camera, let alone find internet access, if she's being held captive by whoever the hell these people are. Could someone be helping her?

I put my pen down and close my journal.

"Do you think Carson from the online form could prove useful?" I ask, sitting on the front porch steps next to Alex.

"Maybe, I mean, he claims he didn't delete that post." Alex says.

"Can we set up a meeting with him?"

"I don't see why not," he says with a shrug. "He already saw the video of her, so it's not a secret to him."

Hot water from the shower loosens my tight muscles. Alison and I often took showers together. The running water relaxed our bodies and cleared our minds; we made it a point to take this time together at least once a week.

The relief of knowing she is alive makes me happy, but the worry of what could happen to her horrifies me. Mindset is everything, and I know these "What if" thoughts aren't helping.

The post removed from the form is suspicious. Is there more to Alison's vanishing? I don't know. The possibilities are endless. Alex must be frustrated with not being able to use his connections in the manner he's used to.

I rinse my body of soap and step out of the shower, dry off with the towel hanging on the rack and get dressed. I look in the mirror my eyes are duller than ever. and sigh before walking out and going back downstairs.

"Are you okay, Alex?"

He tilts his head up from looking at his hands.

"Yes, why?"

"You've been fidgeting with your thumbs and pen."

"Oh, yeah, um… I'm worried for her like you, and I don't know how to do this without help."

"I feel like this is my fault somehow."

"Don't think like that. We will have answers. I don't know when, but we will."

Her parents have yet to be notified of the situation. If they knew about it, they would want to go to the police, something they would do behind my back, even if I ask them not to.

I'll eventually have to visit my in-laws. Keeping this secret from them is eating me alive, but I can't risk the public noticing Alison's case.

What if it makes her situation worse? In most cases, the significant other is the suspect. But how is someone capable of making another person vanish the way she did? She was on the boat one second, her entire being gone the next. There was no splash. She wasn't swimming away. If it were not for her clothes, it would have been as if she had never been there.

It makes little sense and sounds like it came out of a supernatural film, something science fiction. Or maybe this is all just a nightmare. Perhaps I hit my head, and my body is in the hospital suffering from a brain injury.

I shake my head from those thoughts and a memory of what happened once I got home arises.

My hands shake as I unlock the front door. The plane ride back home was a lot longer than when on the way there. It feels like my mind is running a marathon. I slam the door shut behind me. My vision is blurry from crying, my face warm, and my head pounding. I lie back on the couch and cry myself to sleep.

We left to meet Carson the next day after Alex emailed him. It took him half a day to respond, which was torture, but thankfully he did.

Carson lives about two hours away from Missouri and wanted to meet at a cafe. It takes us an hour and a half to get to Springfield, Illinois, the same city, and state where my wife's parents live.

Alex had made sandwiches for the road trip, but I feel sick.

My nerves are getting bad enough that eating seems foreign.

We pull into the cafe and park before heading inside. I look around the dining area and spot a man sitting alone with a computer. We walk toward him.

"Hey, man," I say, offering my hand.

"Hey," Carson shakes mine and Alex's hands, and we sit at the table.

His outfit is casual, black V-neck and jeans. He is taller than me, and I'm 5'10.

"Hey, thank you for coming," I say.

Alex and I don't drink coffee, but this is where Carson wanted us to meet.

"Is there anything you can tell us about the post?" Alex asks, crossing his arms.

Carson opens his laptop and turns it around to show us the screen. "Well, I traced the IP address from the last login, but something is off about it." He points at the screen.

"Here is the location. However, it's just an empty field."

"And that means?" I lean forward as I rest my right arm on the table.

"Long story short, their IP address has been encrypted." He closes his laptop. "Since I'm the admin of the forum, only I can delete the posts. I made sure of that. But I didn't delete it, and that's why I traced the IP address. Someone with high hacking skills must have."

"Is there any way to track an encrypted IP?" I ask.

"It's hard, and it can take time," Carson says.

"We need someone good with computers. Could you help us?" Alex asks.

The cafe only has two employees and a couple of customers aside from us right now. Our voices have been low during this conversation to avoid anyone overhearing us.

"I can," Carson says.

"Great, here is my phone number. We will come to pick you up later today before heading back out," Alex says.

"Woah, what? I thought I would do this remotely."

"Look, if you can't come with us, then we don't need you."

"No, it's alright. I'll be ready when you get me."

Alex and I walk out of the café and head back to the car.

"You need to call Kyle. I know we said we shouldn't get anyone else involved, but this is very important. We need him now."

"I don't know, man. I'm terrified. What if him going to the police hurts Alison?" I ask, fumbling with my phone.

"I don't think he will once we explain."

I sigh, unlock my phone, and press Kyle, my father-in-law's number, to call and let him know we are on our way to visit.

We arrive at my in-laws' house. The summer heat in the country makes me feel a bit on edge. My chest tightens, and my forehead feels wet. I can't tell whether I'm sweating from the heat or feeling nervous about this entire situation.

Alison's parents don't have any neighbors, so they have a lot of land with nothing much on it besides a huge metal shed and a red two-story barn in the back. The house is white and modern, with a large porch and two swings attached to the overhang.

Alex stands beside me as I knock on the door. I can feel my legs shaking.

The door squeaks open, and there stands Alison's dad.

"Jason?" Kyle, my father-in-law, is a barrel-chested man with a bald head and silver-tufted mustache.

"Hi, Kyle. May we come in?" I ask.

"Yes, please, where is Alison?" He seems to be puzzled.

Alex and I walk in. Alex leans against the living room archway and nods for me to explain.

"Something's happened to her," I breathe out. My words come out shaky.

"What do you mean?"

"You're going to want to sit down for this," Alex butts in, and we all sit on the couch.

I explain everything that happened from day one and what we know.

"I thought I could protect her from this," Kyle whispers, as if to himself.

"Uh… protect her from what?"

"Jason, there is so much you don't know."

Kyle's face becomes red. He rubs his forehead with his right hand before standing up. "Come with me."

I look at Alex with wide eyes, and he shrugs as we follow my father-in-law to the basement.

Kyle places his eye in front of a small screen on the door, and it unlocks. I've never been down here before, never had a reason to. I can't wrap my mind around this situation. An iris scanner? Why is this area under strict security?

"How come you use an iris scanner?" I ask.

"It's the safest way I know to keep important things under strict security. I mean, no one else has my eyeballs but me," he laughs.

The door clicks before opening, and we walk inside the room. Two metal tables sit in the middle of the room, with a file cabinet on each end.

"Can you please explain? My wife, your daughter, is missing, and we need to find her."

Kyle narrows his eyes at me before opening a file cabinet with hundreds of papers. He looks through each section before taking out a single yellow file with the number 1010 written on it.

At the sight of those numbers, my mind stops working and my mouth goes dry. I wordlessly look between Alex and Kyle, hoping they pick up on the questions burning in my head.

"These people use software to hide their identity and locations to keep their illegal studies hidden," he says.

He opens the file and hands it to me. Pictures of dark-colored chemical bottles are taped onto the page.

"When Alison was seven, I accidentally left the basement door unlocked. I was downstairs working, and she came to see what I was doing. My boss was looking to create a complicated chemical compound. It was supposedly safe for humans, but that's all I knew." He pauses for a moment before continuing. "She was learning ballet and spun when I told her not to and knocked into the table, which had this chemical sitting on top. It fell on the floor and got on her skin."

Kyle sits down on a metal chair and crosses his arms.

"What does this chemical do, exactly?" I ask, sitting next to him in another chair.

"Have you heard of quantum entanglement?" Kyle asks.

"No," Alex and I say at the same time.

"I found out the people who hired me to work as their chemist wanted to teleport people using two different entangled particles."

"How did you find out?" I ask.

"I didn't find out until after Alison was exposed to them. When she got it on her, I was in the middle of working on it. They knew I'd know eventually and made me sign an NDA before I got the job years prior."

"What does this have to do with her vanishing?" Alex asks, his brows raising from frustration.

"It has everything to do with her vanishing. These people have succeeded at quantum teleportation."

"What the hell is it?" I ask.

"Basically, you have two particles that are connected no matter the distance, and when you interact with one of them, the other connected particle reacts as well." He pauses for a moment and takes a deep breath. I can see sweat coming through his t-shirt.

"Now, what I mentioned is quantum entanglement, but we are dealing with teleportation, which uses a very similar process. Instead of transferring information from one particle to another, it can exchange the two particles with each other."

"So, what you're saying is, my wife is a lab rat?"

Kyle nods without a word.

"Okay, what about the IP address? How do we find her when it's hidden?" I ask.

"It can take a while for an IP address to be decrypted. I might have something better," Kyle says, grabbing the file from my hands and flipping through the pages.

"Didn't you used to work there?" I ask.

"Not at their head location, no. Although, I have a photo here of me and my old boss in front of the place."

"How dangerous are the people she is being held by?" Alex asks.

"Well, it's teleportation… and now that they have succeeded in their goal, I'd say very."

"Teleportation? There's no way this could be happening. How is that possible? Kidnapping people for a future crisis? What the hell were they thinking?" I snap.

All this information is coming in way too fast. My palms sweat, and it's becoming hard to breathe. My heart proceeds to beat faster and faster, and my vision becomes blurry.

"Jason, sit down and take a breather," Kyle says.

I feel his hand touch my shoulder, and I shift away to sit on the floor with my hands over my ears.

"Jason, it's going to be okay," Alex says while wrapping his arm around me.

It wasn't just Alex and me anymore. It was Carson and Kyle, too. At first, Kyle didn't really trust Carson. He knows me and he knows Alex, so of course a random person being in on this worries him. The conversation we had earlier should calm Kyle about Carson a tad bit,

"*How do you know we can trust that guy?*" Kyle grabs his water and takes a sip. "*I mean, he had a video of Alison sent directly to him and he put it on his form instead of sending it to the police.*"

I sigh and glance at Alex, pleading for an answer from him.

"*I know it's weird, but he has skills we need,*" *Alex says.*

"*Skills? What skills?*" *Kyle leans over and places his water back down on the table in front of him before leaning back against the counter, crossing his arms.*

"*Hacking skills, he can get inside remotely,*" *I explain.*

"*I don't know. It seems weird. For all I know, it's another trick from these assholes.*"

"*It's that or we go in without knowing what's ahead,*" *Alex says.*

Kyle looks down for a moment.

"*Alex has a point,*" *I say.*

"*And… if he does something fishy, we could hold him back somehow.*"

An hour went by and all four of us arrived back at my house. We have decided it's best we stay together so that we are all on the same page. Alison's mother knows what is happening but doesn't want to come with us. Kyle called her on the way back, explaining everything.

Her cries broke my heart. Her voice was so loud that everyone in the car could hear her on the phone. Kyle knows he has to keep himself together for his daughter.

The overwhelming feeling of loneliness, hopelessness, worry, and fear because of everything going on is showing underneath my eyes. The last time I shaved was Thursday night, the night before Alison and I left for our honeymoon.

My mirror is foggy from the heat of the shower. I wipe the fog away with my bare hand, but it returns. Distracted, I hadn't noticed how hot the water was running and look down to see that my arms have turned red.

My dark brown hair is desperately in need of a trim. I should clean myself up, or people will think something is wrong with me. Something *is* wrong, but others don't need to know that.

I clean the counter off and throw all the hair I cut away into the trash can. I look up and see Alison's necklace I got her for Christmas last year lying across the jewelry shelf I made for her. I take the chain in my hands, shakily inhale a deep breath, and place it back down. I exhale and slowly walk downstairs.

"Dang, dude, you clean up nice," Alex says, while eating potato chips on the couch.

"People will stare if I don't look presentable."

"Good thinking," he says.

"What's our plan, exactly?" I ask Kyle.

"Well, there's a process. It will be far out with security if this place is where Alison is being held."

He shows me a photo of him in front of a building. The photo is years old, based on how he looks now.

"Where is this?" I ask while crossing my arms.

"Keweenaw Peninsula,"

"In Michigan? Why, of all places?" Alex asks.

"They wanted to hide well, and they have."

"I've heard the peninsula falls off the map sometimes," Alex says, still stuffing his face with potato chips.

"It's because of them," Kyle says.

I look at him with a frown and sit down on the couch.

Michigan's Upper Peninsula is a remote Midwest spot with about eighty percent forest. Beautiful atmosphere. However, they have a map problem, according to Kyle's research. The Keweenaw Peninsula isn't easy to get to, and it's mostly wilderness. It will be challenging to get to Alison, but I'm not backing down and will do everything I can to bring her back.

I sit on the edge of my bed and look down at my feet. The house is quiet. Either everyone is asleep or gone.

I feel useless as a husband right now. Although she is alive, the ache of loss flows through me like a river. I will not cry.

I lie back in my bed and pull the cool, silky top sheet over my warm body. I close my eyes, fighting the tears from brimming. For her, I will be strong. For her, I will not allow others to see my pain. The mountain between us will be no longer. I will have her back home in my arms. No matter what it takes.

<u>SIX</u>

The birds chirping outside the window wake me from a deep slumber. Right now, I have a clear head. I still have questions about these scientists and their plans, but I don't think I'll get those answers anytime soon.

I get up, open the bedroom window, and take a deep breath. The sun is out, and it's a beautiful, warm day. The summer breeze whispers through the trees and comes through the mesh screen. This will be a scary ride, but I'm coming, Alison.

My wife's disappearance finally feels real, and I know I must save her. But it's more than that. Humans shouldn't be messed with like this. I've got to stop these scientists from ever experimenting on anyone like this again.

Kyle feels horrible, although none of this is his fault. All he wanted to do was to protect his daughter. He hid himself and his family for as long as he could, even hoping that burning his house and faking his and his family's deaths years before would stop these people.

He didn't hear anything, which made him think maybe they had given up. It can take scientists a long time to develop something, especially something as insane as teleporting people.

My body shivers from the chills slithering down my spine. Thinking about this horrible situation is making me physically sick. I slip my blue house slippers on before walking out of my bedroom.

When I go downstairs, I don't see Alex in the living room or the other guys. I turn around and then I see Alex outside on the front porch, pacing back and forth, his hand tightly clutching his cell phone.

I open the front door, and he quickly hangs up and puts his phone in his pocket. His face is red.

"Everything okay, Alex?"

"Yes… just issues with… the wife,"

"If you need to go home, I understand."

"No, it's okay. I need to be here for you. She doesn't know the truth about why I'm here. All she knows is that I'm on a business trip. She's a very understanding woman, but impatient."

"Where are Kyle and Carson?" I ask.

"They have been in your office for a while. I've gotta rest my eyes for a bit."

"Oh, okay."

Walking toward my office, I see Kyle looking over some papers and Carson drawing on a tablet for his computer.

"What's going on?" I ask, sitting in my black leather computer chair.

"We are making our own digital and physical map, so we don't need to rely on the normal signal and locations," Kyle says.

"Why is that?"

"Using our own means no signal outages or risk of being taken down if they find out we are there before we get in," Carson says.

"Okay... but what if they can hack it?" I ask.

"I created a system that will notify us if someone is trying, and I can boot them and block their signal before they can get through," Carson says.

I nod, although I am confused by this technology stuff.

We are all in the living room hanging out, trying to prepare for tomorrow as best we can, but we don't know exactly what we're up against. Will there be guards? Will these guards be spread out and hidden in plain sight? We don't know. Kyle only knows so much, as he is just a chemist.

I can't focus on their conversation. I keep thinking about Alison and getting her back.

I don't know what's going to happen once she returns. I don't know if she will be the same Alison.

My bag of clothes are packed and ready to go for tomorrow morning.

<u>SEVEN</u>

It's time. We are on our way to bring Alison home. Another sleepless night. Our alarms went off at 3 am. It's going to take us eleven hours to get there. Fortunately, we can take turns driving when necessary.

Kyle is up first, with his thick dark sunglasses and a baseball cap to avoid being recognized by anyone from the facility. I am wearing a white t-shirt and sitting shotgun. Carson sits behind me. Alex is stuffing his face with potato chips again; he seems to be obsessed with munching on those.

"Alex, are you a nervous eater or something?" Kyle asks.

We have the same thought.

"Don't judge, Mr. Disguise," Alex replies, his tone filled with sarcasm.

The whole car boos at his horrible back talk.

"You seem pretty chill, Jason," Alex says with a mouthful of chips. "I don't get it."

"What do you mean?"

"I mean, you're handling this way better than I could. It's impressive. A little freaky."

I turn to look at him. "Not sure if you're complimenting me or insulting me right now."

Alex doesn't respond immediately, busy cramming more chips into his mouth. There are crumbs on his shirt, already trailing onto the car seat.

I raise an eyebrow and wait for his answer.

"Quit it, guys," Kyle says, glancing at me. He must hear the tension behind my words. "We've got several hours ahead of us, and the last thing I need is to listen to you two bickering."

I face the front again and take a deep breath, trying to calm my nerves. Kyle's right; letting my brother get the best of me right now is stupid.

We leave the city, and that alone feels like we've begun our journey. But with nothing to focus on, I catch myself drifting into all my worries as the countryside passes us by.

What if they're doing things to Alison—awful things? My imagination easily fills my brain with nightmares.

It's been six hours since we've been on the road, and it's time for us to go to a rest stop. Carson has been quiet since we got in the car, and Alex has been asleep since Kyle told him to cut his crap.

We pull in at a rest stop near the highway, an old brick building with two vending machines, one with drinks and another with snacks. A few semis on the exit side of the parking lot, a few cars, a black SUV…

"Oh my god, my legs!" Alex yells.

I stretch my legs on the entrance stairs of the rest stop building. They shake a bit from being in one position for hours. "This feels better." I sigh.

"Dude, chill," Alex says, stretching his arms and legs next to me.

"Look, I don't exercise as much as Alison does. And I've not done a lot since the incident."

"Clearly."

"What's with your attitude, dude?"

"Nothing. I'm fine," he says.

"Guys, six o'clock," Carson whispers, looking behind me with only his eyes.

"What's that mean?"

"Someone is watching us, stupid!" Alex whispers. His tone is deep and aggressive.

I roll my eyes and turn my head to Carson. "How do you know?" I ask.

"Because he's been standing there for the last five minutes, not taking his eyes off you two bickering."

"So, what the hell do we do?" I ask.

"We just act normal, do what we came to this rest stop to do, and let Kyle know when we get to the car," Alex says.

Carson nods in agreement.

"Oh, now you're being helpful," I say.

"Shut up," Alex spits.

"He said to continue to do what we are doing."

"Touché."

Carson shakes his head at us and walks off to the car.

Kyle had been driving us straight to where we needed to be for ten hours, and he didn't want to stop driving, even though all of us said we could take turns. He is a very stubborn man and more determined than ever to bring his daughter back. He knows the ins and outs of these people and what they do.

Kyle takes a different route than the one on the pre-planned map, and we haven't seen the black SUV the man was seen getting into, so we lost him for now. Maybe we are all paranoid, maybe someone isn't actually following us. We are all on edge, no doubt about it.

We pull off the highway onto a gravel back road that kicks up dust behind us as we drive straight north for an extra thirty minutes. Then, we cut left into a deeply wooded area. The distance between driveways to the few houses grows sparse until it feels like we're all alone in the wilderness.

I see a small cabin coming closer to my view.

"Have you always had this place?" I ask.

Kyle puts the car in park. "I built this a few years after the fire. It's always been my and my wife's secret."

I nod and open my door and stand up on the grassy ground. The cabin is deep in the woods. There's no rocky driveway. I hear a loud slam of a car door and look toward it.

"What is your problem, dude?" I ask while looking at Alex. He ignores me and walks toward the cabin.

"Remember the exact location of this place. Otherwise, you'll be lost," he says.

"What is up with your brother's attitude?" Carson asks.

"Hell, if I know. He's been weird since we started the road trip here."

"Huh, maybe he doesn't like long rides."

"Maybe."

EIGHT

Kyle's cabin isn't like anything I've seen before. It's small on the outside, has a timber frame, is dark brown, and is right in the middle of nowhere. Kyle takes his key and puts it into the doorknob, unlocking it and opening it.

This place has trees surrounding every inch of the property. On the inside, it's huge. The flooring is a dark laminated wood that goes through the entire place.

There are two brown leather couches in the living room and a television stand without a television. Two cameras point from the archway of the kitchen toward the door, and one is slightly angled down a small hallway.

I couldn't believe my eyes when I saw a steel door with multiple types of locks on it.

Iris scanner.

High-security padlocks.

Two deadbolts.

Two combination locks.

There are so many things this guy knows… and it frightens me a bit.

The rest of the cabin is… rustic like… old… but this steel door has a small, square window, and I can see stairs leading to a basement. *Creepy, Kyle.*

I step into the bathroom and sit on the floor near the shower. The flooring is ceramic white, rugged and durable, cold tile. Gorgeous, but uncomfortable on my ass.

The fixture produces warm yellow lighting, my least favorite light, but it'll do for now.

I take out my pen and journal from the duffle bag and begin writing.

Hi journal…. not sure if I should even say hi or dear, but here I am. It's been about a month now since Alison vanished. Kyle states that Alison's vanishing has something to do with teleportation.

I never thought something like that could be possible. Kyle is the only reason searching for her has gone faster. Otherwise, it would take longer, especially without being able to get help from the police. Alex has been acting like a jerk since we began our journey to the cabin. I'm not sure why. Maybe being away from his wife and not telling her the real reason he's here is bothering him?

"Jason, hurry. We have things to discuss!" Alex hollers outside the bathroom door.

"Okay!" I read over what I wrote and sigh, closing the little brown notebook and placing it back into the bag. All I want is alone time, just for one moment.

I open the bathroom door and walk toward the living room. Everyone is seated on the couches.

"This place is… insane." I plop myself next to Kyle.

"Because of the location or the steel door?" he laughs.

"Both," I say.

We don't know what move to make next. Alex has been a jerk since we hit the road earlier. I'm starting to think he also feels useless. I mean, he wants to help but doesn't know how without his own connections. Carson also has been quiet doing his own thing, and Kyle has been eyeing him like a hawk, but I don't blame him for not entirely trusting the guy as he doesn't really know him.

"I had created the fire and faked me and my family's death before moving. I figured it would help keep the scientists away for good." Kyle zips open his brown leather bookbag and pulls out a yellow folder with the word **"Certificates."** written in bold letters. "I also thought changing our names would keep them away, but I had to prepare and build that cabin to be safe." He hands me the folder and I open it up, scanning the papers one by one. "I found a house for us to move into far out into the country. The day before I caused the fire, I called a trustworthy close friend from Illinois to help me get our family new names."

My brain feels fuzzy, like static on an old television. Kyle's real name is Ben, and his wife isn't Kayla. It's Victoria. Alison… Ashley?

"Does Alison know?" I ask.

"No, she was too young at the time to understand."

"Why didn't you say something about it when she became an adult?"

"I thought I was protecting her, but I was wrong," he says, placing his hands on his face and rubbing his temples.

"Alison, where are you?" I whisper while walking down a dark hallway. Walls of concrete surround me.

"I'm right here…" her voice is faint.

I turn around, and my eyes widen. She's right in front of me, but I can see right through her.

"Help me, Jason."

My eyes snap open. I throw the blankets off and stand up, wiping my tired eyes. The couch isn't as comfortable as my bed.

"Jason, are you okay?"

I jump at the sudden sound of Kyle's voice. He is standing in the kitchen drinking something out of a mug.

"Yes, another dream of Alison." I lean over and pull a granola bar out of my bag.

"I've been up most of the night. I know where we need to start from here," he says.

"Where are the other two?" I ask, looking around. The kitchen and living room are connected, it's easy to see if someone is in here.

"In the basement, looking over the map for me."

<u>NINE</u>

The map that Carson and Alex have been looking over has directions to the facility.

"What are these?" I ask, pointing at the purple lines going in multiple directions.

"These are escape routes just in case shit hits the fan," Carson says before folding the map.

"I'm hoping nothing goes wrong," I say.

"Dude, something will go wrong. It's a fucking secret guarded facility we will break into," Alex snarls.

His attitude is pissing me off.

"Whatever. Are we going to be walking there? What's the plan?" I ask.

"You'll be on a dirt bike. Alex and I will share a four-wheeler," Kyle's voice echoes around the room, startling me as I didn't hear him come in.

"Since when did you have any of those?"

"Well, if you looked more around the cabin, you'd see I have a shed," Kyle points outside the kitchen window.

"Okay, but what about me? What's my role in this?" Carson says.

"You will be here, hacking into any computer software that they have. Including cameras," Kyle says.

"I'm not sure how I can do that. They are off grid."

"But don't you know how to track their original IP address?"

"Yes, I've been working at it, but it could still take hours."

"Then you better get to it."

While Carson is on hacking duty, I'm looking over the camo-painted dirt bike in the shed. With the cabin built with multiple high-security locks on a basement door, the front door having an iris scanner, cameras surrounding the house and cabin, and now the four-wheeler and dirt bike, Kyle has been fully prepared just in case something happens to his daughter, my wife, for a long time.

Kyle leaves with two big gas cans to fill the four-wheeler and dirt bike. The closest gas station is thirty minutes away.

I walk into the shed. It's just a regular small barn shed that I've seen in many big hardware retailers.

Dark brown exterior, wooden floors. Nothing top security about this. Two deer heads are mounted like decorations and a fifty-pound flathead catfish is mounted on the wall across from the deer.

This man is a hunter.

"Ready to go?" Kyle says.

I look at him with wide eyes. I didn't realize he was back.

"Yes."

"I have three duffle bags packed and a bookbag for the trip." He hands me a duffle bag, and I open it up to see a walkie-talkie, granola bars, matches, and a hand towel.

"No weapons?" I ask.

"They are in the bookbag. Let's go get Alex and head out."

I haven't driven a dirt bike in a long time, not since I was a boy. Before my parents moved us to Missouri, my best friend at the time owned one, and we drove it around the block during the weekends or after class and all summer long. I miss those days. Unfortunately, I didn't get to say goodbye to him. Jensen was at school the day I moved. I haven't spoken to him since.

Driving in the woods is calming.

My mind wanders to Alison. I miss stroking her blonde wavy hair while holding her in bed. The scent of vanilla on her neck always places a smile on my face. Thinking about doing it again brings goosebumps all over my body…

The woods have a slight breeze when driving through them, bringing my mind back to the present. The facility is ten more miles away, but we will camp out at three miles and walk the rest of the way.

There is no way we could have walked the entire distance because our energy would be low as hell, and we need to get to Alison with a clear head and be fully awake.

Kyle and Alex are driving in front of me on the four-wheeler. Alex is on the lookout. His private investigator skills will help us out a lot. He will tell us if there are guards or anything suspicious for me and Kyle to be aware of. Kyle and I will fight to get in and possibly bring down a few guards if needed.

A short while later, Kyle pulls into a cleared area of the woods, relatively small, but big enough for us to camp in. This is a heavily forested area with birch, maple, and oak trees. The entire region is crisscrossed with forest roads, but there's miles of snowmobile trails, and during the summer, deer hunters come through with four-wheelers.

"Alright, Jason, go find some log for us to sit on. Alex, you look around our surroundings and make sure we are in the clear," Kyle says.

"What are you doing?" I ask.

"I am going to talk to Carson with the walkie-talkie and see where he's at with hacking their system." Kyle says and walks away for a moment. Minutes go by, and I look up to see Kyle walking back toward me.

"Carson is in," Kyle says.

"Really?" I stand up from the log I found and walk toward him.

"Yes, he has access to the cameras and files."

"Holy shit, that's awesome," Alex says, while taking a bite of his granola bar.

"Is Carson going to update us, or are we going to call him when we need him?"

Kyle looks up from his notepad. "We will ask for him. It's the safest way so that no one hears us at the times we need to be quiet," he says.

He places his notepad down and picks up the black bookbag from beside him, opening it.

"Do you know how to shoot?" Kyle asks, glancing at Alex and me.

"Not really, but I know of them," I say.

"Yes, I was trained with them." Alex says.

"Okay, Jason, do you see this switch?" Kyle says.

"Yes."

"That is safety. Swipe this to the left to expose this red. Remember, red for dead. The safety is now off. Swipe it right to switch it off," he says and holds the gun out.

"Establish your grip, keep your index finger stiff here, hand up on the grip, all the way to the beaver's tail as high as you can get it. Wrap your other fingers just under the trigger. Only move your index when ready to shoot."

He hands me the gun.

"To check if it's loaded, use your right thumb and press this button. This is the magazine release. It'll fall out, and you can see if it's loaded." He rests the magazine down on his leg.

"To make sure your chamber is empty, establish a firing grip as I showed you; pull this back all the way, and you can see that it is empty. Practice holding it for a bit. Do what I did with safety, and you will be prepared for anything that happens."

Hey, journal, it's me again. Me, Alex, and Kyle are at the campsite… more like a random cleared spot in the woods. There are maple trees around me, my favorite kind of tree. I learned to hold and use a gun, which is something I never expected I'd ever have to do, but once all of this is over, I might just get one to protect my wife and me and keep it locked away in a safe.

The sounds of cicadas and crickets surround me. Kyle lit a small fire once we settled in the camp, which was four hours ago. It's now nearing midnight. Kyle suggested we wait until midnight before we walk the rest of the three miles to get to the facility, which makes sense. We need our energy full, our stomachs decently filled with the snacks we brought, and try to take a catnap before we leave.

I'm unsure of what's going to happen in the next moments…

I place my notepad down.

Instead of sleeping, I've been obsessively thinking about being moments away from seeing my wife and bringing her back home. Scaring myself with thoughts I shouldn't have… Is she still alive?

Is she okay?

I can't do this thing called life without her.

My thoughts run like I'm running a marathon.

"Let's move," Kyle says.

TEN

From what I know, this facility is in an underground bunker, which is a perfect spot to hide, especially in the middle of the woods. It's dark and extremely hard to see, but even during the day, I'm sure it's hard to spot unless you know exactly where it's at.

"Shit, the digital map broke!" Kyle kicks a rock in front of him. "Gotta use the paper map." He sighs and pulls it out of his back pocket. The moon barely gives us light to see. He pulls a lighter out of his pocket and switches it on.

"Okay, guys, based on what the map shows, we are half a mile away from the bunker." He pauses for a moment. "This red mark is where the bunker is. These blue lines are the surrounding areas where guards could be."

"Okay, but how are we going to know where they are? We can't just go in without getting caught," I say.

"Alex, go look around the perimeter now. We are nearing the bunker, and we'll need cover soon," Kyle commands.

Alex adjusts his duffle bag and nods, walking the other way.

"Okay, what cameras does Carson have access to?" I ask.

"All. Inside and out." Kyle grabs his walkie-talkie and holds it close to his mouth. "Carson, do you copy?"

There's silence for a moment.

"Yes," Carson whispers.

"Check the outside cameras and the inside of the front door."

There's a slight pause. I crack my knuckles, patiently waiting but tired of it. I've been waiting for weeks to see Alison.

"Okay, there's one guard near the front outside and one on each side of the building. I don't see any more than that."

"This will be easier than I thought then. Thanks, Carson. If we don't communicate within the next hour, run, and call my wife," Kyle says, putting the walkie-talkie back into his bag.

"Did you seriously just say that?"

"Better to be safe than sorry, Jason. You'll learn."

As we get closer to the bunker, my stomach feels hollow, and I wrap my arms around myself. There's so much happening, but I've got to be brave for my wife. I've got to be there for her.

Tree branches move slowly from the breeze. I take a deep breath and try to calm my nerves.

I pull out the thermal goggles from my belt and look through them. The front door guard has a plate carrier with spare magazines on the front and a duty belt with a pistol on one side and magazines on the other.

Kyle runs toward the other side of the building, deep in the trees, while I keep my eye on the first target and slowly walk toward him.

The guard turns in my direction, but I quickly hide behind a tree and duck to avoid getting caught. I take a deep breath and hear my heart pounding in my chest.

Slowly, I stand back up and peek around the tree. I lift my thermal goggles to my eyes and see the guard facing the opposite of me and listen as he whistles for no reason other than boredom.

If I don't hurt him, I may never have the chance to see my wife again. Going home without her would put me in a place of anger and rage, the opposite of who I already am. Her not being in my arms would crush every nerve and bone inside me, along with every bit of my heart and soul.

I close my eyes and recall the memory I have of holding Alison in my arms the first night we moved into our house. Her laughter fills the empty place we just shoved a couch and bed in.

"I can't wait to see our little ones running around here one day." *She leans in to hug me.*

I place my arms around her waist and pull her into a tighter embrace.

"Let's hope they don't have your awful cooking skills," I say while looking into her blue eyes.

She lifts her hand and taps me on the back of the head. "Shut up, bozo!"

I laugh and give her a kiss.

"Pizza night?"

I open my eyes, and as I take a deep breath, I hold my knife tightly. I sprint toward the guard, the sound of leaves crunching with every step I take, and just as the guard turns, I tackle him to the ground.

In the heat of the moment, he is surprised and tries to get to his gun. I straddle his abdomen and, while he is fumbling for his weapon, I shove my free hand into his face to keep him quiet. Without hesitation, I stab him multiple times, losing track of how many, into what feels like his left armpit and upper ribs.

After what seems like an eternity, the guard struggles less, eventually succumbing to his wounds, and his body goes limp.

I stand and lean against a tree nearby. My body trembles as I look at my bloody hands, barely able to see them in the moonlight. My heart pounds, and all I can smell is the metallic tang of blood. I cannot believe I just did that…I've learned about knives from my uncle and have watched some movies that involve fighting but I have never been in a fight myself…call it luck, I guess…

I hear a static noise coming from the guard's pocket. I crawl over to him and reach into his pocket… a walkie-talkie.

"Roger, do you copy? What was that noise?" A deep voice speaks through.

Shit, I have to do something.

I bring the walkie-talkie toward my mouth and take a deep breath before speaking.

"Yes, I copy. Nothing but a damn squirrel," I say, hoping the other guy on the line believes me.

A moment of silence goes by.

"Ah, nothing else to do out here besides guard. At least you had fun."

Yeah, *fun*.

After turning the volume down, I put the walkie-talkie in my back pocket and pat around the now dead guard's body to locate a key. I feel a plastic card in his pants pocket, along with corrugated keys. Jackpot.

With my legs shaking, I grab his pistol, placing it into my duffle bag and stand up to walk toward the door, placing the key swipe in the slot. A green light appears on the keypad, and the door cracks open.

Kyle and Alex aren't inside with me. They are taking out the other guards.

The lights are on but slightly dimmed. Narrow concrete walls surround me. I look down and see blood covering my entire right hand and splatters of it on my forearm, shirt, pants, and shoes.

I stumble down the hallway with a heavy breath, blood pumping through my body, and my head spinning. *What is going on with me?* I think to myself.

The ear-piercing sound of nails scratching a wall is coming from behind one of the four metal doors I stop in front of.

A knob jiggles on one of them. I quickly hide behind a wall with a dark corner and no light. My back leaned against it, and I turn my head to the side.

"Patient 1010 is ready for testing," a male voice says.

1010… Alison!

"No, we need a few more days," a second male's voice replies.

"We don't have a few days. Get your shit taken care of now." The first male voice sounds old, wicked.

"Yes, sir!"

Footsteps head in the opposite direction from me. I let out a breath once I realize no one is there anymore.

Looking around the corner of this wall, I see that the metal door is closed, but it has the same style lock as the front door of the building.

I step slowly toward the door they exited from and peek through the small glass window. There are plain white walls and tile flooring with empty hospital beds and IV infusion machines next to each.

With a look behind me to be sure no one is there, I hurry to unlock the door with the swipe card.

ELEVEN

This room is just as clean as a hospital room—no garbage, nothing unorganized or out of place. The only light in the room is L.E. D. lights underneath cabinets, and the ceiling light is turned off.

I walk toward a hospital bed, sit, and pull out my walkie-talkie.

"Kyle, are you there?" I whisper while I keep looking around my surroundings, making sure I am in the clear and not caught.

"Yes, one more guy down, and we will be inside."

"I'm already in," I say.

"What!" he yells into the walkie-talkie.

I squint at the sudden loudness of his voice and turn the volume dial down.

"How the fuck did you get in so fast?" he asks.

"Anger came over me. I took out the guard in a way I never expected to." I stutter my words, looking at my bloody hands.

"There's people that'll be inside, so remember, red means dead."

"I got it. See you shortly." I turn the volume down even more and put the walkie-talkie back in my pocket.

I take a deep breath, stand up, and walk toward the counters. The cabinets have no locks. I open one, and nothing but medical supplies such as needles, thermometers, stethoscopes, and band-aids sit inside, spotless and organized well. They are categorized as M.A.

Initials maybe?

Nothing useful is in them.

I open a drawer and see a chart. I tilt my head to the side, pick it up, and place it on the counter so I can get good lighting to read it better.

DOCUMENTATION FOR M.A.

PATIENT 1001

Patient 1001 has been an unpleasant experience. We could transport the patient, but only partial parts of the body came to us. We could not do further testing.

PATIENT 1002

Patient 1002 was in worse shape than patient 1001. Gory details I'd rather not explain.

Oh, my god… I shake my head when looking at photos of the patients attached to the chart.

I put everything back into the drawer and hold myself up against the counter with my hands, trying not to collapse from the things I've read and seen already.

A loud bang echoes throughout the building.

"What the hell?" I whisper.

As another loud bang echoes, I grab my gun and walk toward the exit door.

I grab the door handle and slowly open the door enough to peek my head through to see what's going on. I don't see anything, but I hear voices.

"We need to find Jason." It was Kyle's voice.

I hurry and walk to where I heard him.

"I'm right here," I whisper.

Kyle turns and looks at me with wide eyes.

"Oh, you're okay, good. Damn, you are a mess," he says, referencing my blood-stained outfit and hands.

"Yes, I know."

"Have you found anything about Alison yet?"

"No, but I found some documents from other patients. They aren't great to look at, and I heard people talking about her being an experiment."

"Go grab the documents and put them in your bag."

"What? Why?" I ask.

"We need evidence if we are going to shut these guys down."

I nod and walk back into the room, but as I do so, a man with a white lab coat and wide eyes is looking at me.

"Who are you? How did you get in?" His voice is raised, but his words come out shaky.

"Where's my wife?" I yell while pointing my gun at him.

The door behind me opens and Kyle enters.

The man lifts his hands and freezes.

"What the hell?" Kyle pulls a rope from his bag and walks toward the man.

"I'm going to tie your hands behind your back, and you are going to answer every question we have. Do you understand?" Kyle says.

I continue pointing my gun at the man while Kyle ties him up and pushes him to sit on the edge of one of the hospital beds.

"W-who is your wife?" the man says.

"Alison Kendrick. Now, where is she?"

"I don't know anyone named Alison."

His answer frustrates me. I take my gun and rest it on the bottom of his chin.

"Okay, patient 1010. Where is she?"

His eyes widen. "She's being prepped for a last test." I can see tears forming in the corners of his eyes.

"Where at in the building, goddammit?" I push him back and place one hand around his neck. With my other hand, I press the barrel of the gun against his temple. "Fucking answer me."

"Sh-she is on the fifth floor of the bunker," he says.

"How do I get there?"

"Follow the signs!"

I can see the sweat dripping from his temples as his breathing becomes heavy. I let go of his neck and stand up straight while still aiming the gun at him.

"But you'll need security clearance to access those levels," he says.

I pull the swipe card from my pocket and bring it close to his face. "Will this work?"

"Yes, that is an access key, but I don't know what clearance level it has."

"Okay, Kyle, what do we do with him?"

"Well, either kill him or let him go and tell someone."

"I don't want to kill someone again..."

Kyle sighs and looks at the man, whose hands are tied behind his back. He walks around the room, looking for something, then grabs his gun from his pocket and shoots the man in the head.

I stumble backwards, the loudness of the gun making my ears ache. My head feels fuzzy.

"Let's go," Kyle barks.

TWELVE

My ears are ringing from the sudden shot Kyle made, but the dizziness went away a couple of minutes after walking around the narrow hallways of the bunker.

There are stairs at the end of the hall, and there have been no guards to come up or come in from anywhere. Why aren't there any alarms going on after the gunshot?

I look over at Kyle. His entire right side is covered with dirt and grass mixed with blood. "What happened out there?" I ask.

"It wasn't as bad as your fight clearly was," he says, looking me up and down.

He pulls out his walkie-talkie from his back pocket. "Carson, do you copy?" he whispers.

"Yes, I'm here."

"Is there anyone behind these doors, lower level three?"

"No, no one."

"Please watch every camera we come close to and the ones that we pass through afterwards."

"On it."

Kyle puts his walkie-talkie back into his pocket.

Upon reaching level four, I take out the swipe card and breathe deeply.

Kyle nods at me to continue, and I insert the key and pull it out quickly. The door makes a beep sound, and a little green light appears before a clicking noise.

I look at Kyle with a nod before opening the door of level four.

Level four isn't the same as levels one and three. These halls have no tile flooring. The ceiling and floor are gray concrete, no windows, and with dim lighting. It's mostly dark through here.

"Okay, Carson, is there anything behind this level-four door?" Kyle asks.

There was almost a minute of silence.

"There are two guards on each side of the hall. No more after that."

"Okay," Kyle says before putting the walkie-talkie down.

"What's the plan? We can't just walk in without getting killed."

"You aim left. I aim right."

I shake my head, the nerves in my body have left. It's like I am numb, frozen from any feelings from the adrenaline pumping through my body.

My head throbs from the worries of what happened to him since he is not here with Kyle and me. I shake the thoughts from my head and insert the key. No beep sound was made this time, but a red light appears.

Fuck.

An alarm blares throughout the bunker, and the lights dim, making the hallway almost entirely dark.

"Go down that way. I'll go this way. The moment you hear steps, shoot," Kyle whisper-yells.

I run toward the end of the hallway where we came from to reach level four. All doors have a red light, making me wonder if security has been tightened after the alarm. The only way I will win this and get my wife back is if I play it smart.

I crouch in the corner and take out my duffle bag. I've done this in the dark, so I can do this now. Before throwing the bag back on, I felt around for my goggles.

I hear steps coming from behind the entrance door. I put the goggles over my eyes and see the door open. One guard peeps through, pointing his military-grade gun in front of him. I take a deep breath and aim for his head, but my hand is shaky. I can't do this with one hand.

While keeping my eyes straight, I quietly place the goggles down and focus on the guard in front of me. Gripping the gun with my other hand, I place my right finger on the trigger and pull it.

The echo of the gun is louder than the alarm, and I hear the guard fall to the ground.

I grab my goggles and look through them. I got him exactly where I needed to. Blood pools from his head.

"Jason, are you okay?" Kyle's voice is loud, but the sound of the alarms ringing from the speakers drowns him out.

I run toward the guard, take out his key, grab his gun, and run toward the other door.

"Come on!" I command Kyle.

I insert this key, and it goes through. This key must be an emergency access one.

I push through, noticing the lights are brighter once I enter level four. Every hallway leads to the next level.

There are no guards here anymore, and Kyle is right behind me. My breath is heavy, my body is covered with sweat, and the shaking of my limbs has disappeared. We are getting closer to saving my wife.

"Stay behind me," Kyle says.

"Okay."

He hurries in front of me and walks slowly toward the stairs, his body close to the wall, the same as mine. He places his back against it, holds the gun up toward the ceiling right in front of his face, then turns his torso and head to look around the corner.

The gun goes off. Kyle runs down the stairs. "Stay," he orders me.

I stay put. My heart thumps hard against my chest. I feel it might jump out.

One… the gun echoes. Two… another. Three…

I run down the stairs with my gun pointing straight in front of me. Kyle is on the ground, holding his hand over his chest. I approach him and crouch.

"Kyle, you're going to be okay."

I don't have any medical supplies, but I check his bag, and not much to my surprise, he has bandages.

I rip his shirt with my bare hands. There is a bullet wound right in his upper shoulder with no exit wound.

Kyle looks up at me with tears in his eyes. "I won't make it."

"No, you're going to be fine."

I place the bandages over the wound, applying a lot of pressure with my hands while tying the piece of his shirt around his shoulder as tightly as I can.

"Jason, stop."

Ignoring him, I drag him to the wall and prop him against it.

He looks at me and grabs my arm. "Jason, go get Alison," he wheezes.

My head is spinning. I can't leave him here. This situation is messed up.

"I have a gun and everything I need to defend myself. You can do this," he says. "All that matters is that we get her out of here. Stop wasting your time and hurry." His voice cracks while speaking every word.

I look behind me and grab the gun that I took from the guard.

"Keep this on you." I set it on his lap, and he puts his hand on it.

"Alex did this," he says.

I stare at him. "Did you hit your head?" I ask, my stomach in knots.

Kyle shakes his head.

"Are you sure you will be fine?"

"Go."

After giving him a nod, I stand up and head toward level five.

I'm here, Alison. I'm coming to save you.

THIRTEEN

The other side of this door on level five could have Alison—or something else. My hand is shaking when I reach for the door. I slide the key into the lock while the red light is still on, and suddenly, the door opens without me touching it.

As I step through, I put the key back into my pocket and grip my gun in front of me. Not a single person is in sight, as I look from left to right. I sigh and reach for the walkie-talkie.

I press the talk button. "Carson, are you there?"

"Yes, is everything okay?"

"Kyle is down. He's been shot."

"What? Holy shit!"

"I need your help. Can you locate Alex on any cameras?"

"Let me check them,"

Kyle needs to survive. He needs to see his daughter.

"I don't see him anywhere," Carson says.

"What do you mean?" I lean against a wall and scratch the back of my neck.

"The last I saw was him covering up a camera."

I tilt my head. That doesn't seem like something he'd do.

"Where at?"

"Inside, level seven."

My eyes widen, and I freeze for a moment. There's no reason for him to be that far down. How the fuck did he even get down there without me seeing him?

"Okay, Carson, are you sure it was him?"

"Yes."

"Alright, are there any guards between level five and seven?"

"I don't see any, but Alison is there. She was being taken to another room. I tried to say something, but those alarms were on, and they were too loud for you to hear me."

"*FUCK!*" I scream and kick the concrete wall in front of me. "What the hell! *Fuck!*" My voice cracks when I yell out. I inhale a deep breath and close my eyes. I exhale and repeat two more times, trying to calm myself down. Alex is here, but there are so many rooms. Carson has no room access... wait...

Looking up at the ceiling, I bring the walkie-talkie close to my mouth.

"C-carson?" I stutter. My breath is shaky.

"Yes?"

"Can you tell me what room she went in?"

"She is still on level five, but there are no cameras pointing the way she went. Go left from the door you entered from. You will see cameras, then where there is none is where she could be."

"Thanks, man. We aren't done here yet."

I turn the volume down and put the walkie-talkie back into my pocket as I stand back up.

Two cameras are pointing toward me on the left side where Carson said to go. When I walk past them and down the steps, I hear heavy footsteps coming in my direction. I stay put and hold my breath.

A man with gray hair and a blue lab coat appears before me. He turns and notices me, and before he makes a sound, I tackle him to the ground and place him in a chokehold.

He grabs my arm with both hands and tries to pull me off, but I hold tighter, and soon enough, he stops fighting me.

I let out a breath and push him off me. He's not dead, at least I don't think so, but I do not care at this point. He and the other workers in this building will pay for what they have been doing to others, especially my wife.

Feeling around his lab coat, I take out a key from his pocket. This is just a flat corrugated silver key, nothing close to a security access key. I put it in my pocket and continue searching.

I fumble through the left pocket and pull out something thin plastic—a photo.

"Jamie, 2020." I read aloud the words written on the back.

I flip the image.

My eyes widen. The face looks very familiar. I bring it closer to my eyes. The man in the photo is in front of a building, and not just any building—the Hard Rock Hotel Alison and I were staying at. Jamie, the receptionist.

I shake my head and look up at the man passed out on the floor.

I stand up and put the photo in my pocket. Alex and I do not know what happened to Jamie; all we know is that he vanished the same way Alison did.

But we didn't think much about it.

If this man is holding onto an image of Jamie… no, it can't be.

I walk down the stairs without looking back at the older gentlemen. It's time to get Alison out of here.

I run toward the end of the hall and use the swipe key on a metal door. The light turns green, but it doesn't unlock. Fuck.

I kick the lock multiple times as hard as possible, and the door finally opens. I push through and slam the door behind me. This isn't a hallway. This room also isn't like the other rooms that I have been in.

The walls are painted gray with no decorations of any kind. I look around the room. There's a metal table with a dark blue plastic clipboard lying on top with a metal garbage can underneath. A bulky microscope machine is next to the clipboard, and a blood pressure cuff is mounted on the wall. I turn from the table, and suddenly, I am frozen in place. I can feel beads of sweat rolling down my forehead.

A woman is lying on a hospital bed covered in white bedsheets, and wires dangling from machines are attached to her temples. Stepping closer to her, I inhale a sharp breath.

I blink, hoping this is all a dream. My heart races when I get to her bedside. Her once beautiful, glowing face has become dull, like she hasn't slept for weeks. I exhale the breath I was holding when I notice her chest moving. She's *alive*.

I hold Alison's hand to my chest and lean to kiss her forehead and her eyes start to twitch.

"I love you. I found you. I'm here, baby. I will get you out of here. Just hold on," I whisper.

I caress her cheek and kiss her forehead again, staring at her for a moment.

Her eyes flutter open, and she looks around until she sees me.

"Jason?"

FOURTEEN

"I'm here, Alison, I'm here."

"What's going on? How did you get inside?" her speech was slurring, they must have given her something.

I take a deep breath and sit on the bed next to her.

"That doesn't matter right now. We need to get you out of here."

I look at the machine. It looks like it's collecting data from her brain.

"I'm scared," she says.

Alison's voice is shaking, and my heart feels like it's being torn apart. I stand back up, take the wires off her temples, and toss them to the ground.

"Don't be." I look at her. She's not sat up since her eyes opened. "Can you walk?"

"They drugged me to keep me calm for the data to read correctly. If I walk, I'll look drunk."

I nod and throw the sheets off her and notice she is in a hospital gown. I lean down and push my hand between the bed and her back to lift her. She slowly turns her waist, and her legs go over the edge.

I hold her hand so she can use me as support, and one foot at a time, she slowly stands up.

She tilts her head up at me. "I knew you'd come for me."

"Let's get out of here."

I pick her up into my arms, and just as we exit the room, the alarm goes off again, but this time it's different. White lights flash in every corner of the room, which I assume is a triggered fire alarm.

I hurry to open the door, and we leave the way I came.

As I run to level four, clouds of smoke rush toward us. I set Alison down and rip the bottom of my shirt, making a strip of cloth to place over Alison's nose and mouth. I do the same for myself. Before I run the opposite way, I lift her back into my arms. The other way leads us to an emergency exit. I place my back on the door to push the wide metal button to open it, but it doesn't budge.

Alison coughs.

"Hold on, baby. We are so close." I place her down once again and take out my walkie-talkie, bringing it close to my mouth. "Carson, help! Fire and smoke are heading my way. I need a way out of here."

"There is an emergency exit door in the room Alison was in."

I shove the walkie-talkie back into my pocket and pull the swipe key out of my other pocket, lifting her into my arms and running back. The door is locked. I insert the key, and it clicks.

I kick the door open and run to the end of the room. EXIT is spelled out in big red letters above it. How come I didn't see this before?

When running down another hallway, Alison lifts her head and gasps.

I stop in my tracks. "What?"

I look at her, eyebrows furrowed.

"Was that Alex?" She points into the room we passed to the left.

My eyes widen.

I turn and step towards the room she pointed at, and to my ultimate surprise, Alex is holding a knife in his hand, blood dripping from the blade. He doesn't have a single sign of struggle on his body, no dirt, no cuts, no blood.

His back is facing me as I stand in the door frame. A man with a black t-shirt and blue jeans is lying on the ground in front of him, blood pooling around his head.

"What the fuck did you do, Alex?" I yell.

He jumps and quickly turns to face me, paler than the color of white itself. His brows raise, his eyes widen, and his mouth drops.

"Say something!"

"Jason… that's Jamie from the hotel," Alison says.

"What?" I look at the face, and sure enough, it's Jamie.

"I can explain," Alex says, rushing toward me as I back up.

"Explain what? You just killed an innocent man!"

Alex throws his arms in the air and leans against the wall next to him.

"He was going to tell someone about me!"

"About you? What is there to tell?" My voice raises, and I can feel my face becoming hot and flushed.

He opens his mouth, but water splashes onto us. The sprinklers have finally turned on.

"Let's go, *now!*"

I run back down the hallway to where I was trying to leave. Alex is right behind us.

"I'll explain everything!" I hear his voice, but it's faded, the alarm and water drowning him out.

My breathing quickens and sweat comes through areas I never thought I could sweat from. My clothes are now drenched with water.

Every step of the way feels harder. The stairs are long, but the light at the end of the tunnel is near.

By the second floor, I am still coughing from inhaling the smoke, but I don't care, at least the water from the sprinklers has cleared it all out. I rush toward level one, and I stop in my tracks. The person I didn't expect to see in front of the main doors is Kyle. I didn't see him get down here, he must have found another door, there's so many of them.

He's standing with his hand resting on the open door.

"Go!" his voice is deep.

I shake my head and run out the door.

It's still dark, but the sun is just beginning to rise. The four-wheeler and dirt bike are a couple miles away. Shit!

The muscles in my legs cramp. Alison is still in my arms, but her eyes are closed.

"Baby girl, stay awake. We are almost there!" I urge her.

Her eyes flutter open. "Where is there?"

"Home."

Finally, I get to the dirt bike. The seat is long enough for both of us to fit. I set her down first, and I get behind her.

"*Jason! Go! Go! Go!*" Kyle yells after us.

I see him approaching the four-wheeler, and Alex is running behind him. My arms ache from the fighting, running and lifting I've had to do. I look behind Alex and notice two men running toward him. Two loud echoes spread throughout these dense woods. *Shit.*

The men fall back. I look at Kyle. He has a gun pointing straight at the men. I look at the men one more time as the engine of the bike roars, and I hurry Alison and me back to the cabin.

When we arrive at the cabin, I hop off the bike and take her in my arms before we run inside. I lay her down gently on the couch. She's still out of it.

"Where are we?"

"Your dad's cabin."

"My dad has a cabin?"

Almost like it's on cue, the door bursts open, and Kyle comes stumbling in the door. His body is drenched with water, his face is dirty with blood, and he has minor cuts on his jawline.

"Don't let Alex inside," he says before nearly falling to the floor.

I rush to his side and place his good arm over my shoulder as I guide him into the kitchen and sit him down on a chair.

"Carson! Grab the first aid kit and some hand towels!" I holler.

I hear loud footsteps running up the basement stairs, and the door flies open. I look up from Kyle's bullet wound and see Carson with arms full.

"Here!" he says, setting it onto the table with some alcohol.

I use the scissors from the first aid kit and cut Kyle's shirt off. He's mumbling slurs of pain. I grab the hand towel and add pressure over his wound and rip open the bandages. Carson grabs the rubbing alcohol and spills it over the wound.

"*Ouch!* That fucking hurts!" Kyle cries out in pain.

"I'm sorry man," Carson says.

Kyle looks at Carson, then me, and closes his eyes.

"The bullet is inside. We need real medics."

Carson types into his phone. "The closest hospital is just under an hour away."

I sigh and turn, brushing my hair back with both hands as I turn to face him. "Then call and tell them to meet us halfway."

The front door bursts open, and I quickly turn and see that it's Alex.

I take a deep breath, push past Carson, and march toward Alex.

"What the fuck do you want?" My voice is raspy. I glare at Alex as I shove him out the front door with both hands. "Huh? What game are you playing, fucker?" I snarl.

Thunder roars, and rain sprinkles on top of us.

Alex raises his arms in defense. "It's not what you think, man."

"You have been betraying me this entire time. Is that why there was a delay in searching for her? And your attitude on the way here?" My entire body is burning up from the overwhelming rage inside.

"They threatened me. I didn't know what to do!"

I grab him by the collar and lift him to his feet.

"What?" With every word I say, spit comes out of my mouth. I've never felt such anger in my entire life. "Who?" I stare at him with my fists clenched to my sides.

"Those science freaks! They came to me and told me they needed help to find Kyle. If I didn't help you get there, they would've killed me, Marissa, Alison, and you!"

He holds his hand to his chest while breathing heavily, and I look at him, disgusted and confused.

"Jason, let's go!" I turn and see Carson taking Kyle to the car.

I nod and turn back to face Alex, looking him up and down to see that there are no weapons on him. "You can stay here."

"What?" he asks.

"You heard me. We will discuss this later!" I walk to the car and open the back door. "You're going to be okay, Kyle," I say and help him into the seat.

I run back inside and rush toward Alison. Sliding my left arm under her back and my other under her knees, lifting her close to my chest. Her body is limp from being drugged. I walk back to the car, setting her down next to her dad.

I look at Alex through the windshield. He's crying, his face is blotchy, and his body is trembling. The rain is cold, but Alex never cared for rain.

I buckle Alison in next to her dad. "I'll be right back."

"What are you doing?" Carson asks.

"Taking care of this." I slightly nudge my head toward Alex and Carson slowly nods.

Walking back to my brother, I put my hand out in front of him. He looks up at me; his eyes are red and blinking a lot.

My breathing is slowing down, but my body is still shaking. The slower my breathing becomes, the stronger my heart feels.

Alex takes my hand, and I lift him. As soon as I do so, I notice something fall from his pocket onto the mud and grass. It's shiny, like silver. I reach down to grab it and see that it's a lighter. We didn't have lighters in the duffle bags, only Kyle had one.

I lift my hand, holding the lighter between my thumb and index fingers. "Why do you have this?"

Alex looks down at his feet.

"Damn it, Alex. My wife is in the car with some sort of drug in her system, and my father-in-law is on the brink of dying. Fucking tell me!"

"I caused the fire," he blurts out.

"Why? Were you trying to kill us all?"

"No."

"Then why hurt Kyle? Why light the building on fire?"

"I hurt him… to pretend I was on their side."

"Who's side?"

"The people her dad worked for."

I put the lighter in my front pocket.

"I can't right now."

Alex tries to turn me around by grabbing my shoulder. "Stop, please let me explain!"

I shove him to the ground. This time, he falls hard and cries out, holding his ankle. "Fuck you, dude."

FIFTEEN

It's been a week since everything went down. I walk through the hospital doors with Alison beside me. I've not spoken to Alex since I found out about his betrayal. He gave his excuse, but I'm not sure if I buy it.

The hospital in Michigan transferred Kyle to Memorial Hospital in Springfield, Illinois. I've refused to face Alex and stayed by Alison's side. The most important person in the world is finally back in my arms.

I take her hand in mine and kiss it gently before we sit on the brown leather chairs of the hospital room where Kyle rests during his recovery.

"What have the doctors said?" I ask, leaning forward, resting my elbows on my knees, and clasping my hands together.

"I'll need some physical therapy after having a sling for a few weeks, but I'll be okay," he says, shrugging his good shoulder.

"Daddy, I don't understand why this happened."

"We can't speak about it here." He puts his index finger up to his lips, shushing her.

"Have the cops come in yet?" I ask.

"They did a few hours ago. I didn't tell them much besides that it was a freak accident with my gun."

"And they bought that?"

"Hopefully. I stayed calm, and that may have convinced them enough."

Alison nods, then looks at me. "Where is Carson?"

"Carson decided to hunt for security jobs."

"Really?" Kyle asks, his voice full of sarcasm.

I chuckle.

Carson did well with watching out for us and keeping a lookout remotely. He decided that a security job that included technology was something he wanted to be paid to do.

"You guys should go back home. I am going to be fine."

"I'm not going home until I know everything is okay," Alison says.

"Just go back and see your mom so she can explain everything to you." He gives Alison a pleading look, and his bottom lip pokes out a little. "The house keys are in my jean pocket." He points across the room. I look over and see his old clothes in a plastic bag sitting on a chair.

"Okay, stop with the pouty face," she says, standing to lean in and then kissing her dad's forehead and hugging him.

Kyle pats her back, and she lets go. "I'll be fine," he says.

Alison smiles and looks at me, holding out her hand.

"See you later, Kyle," I say.

I take Alison's hand, and we walk out of the room.

"Do you think they will come back for me?" she asks.

"I don't know…"

Twenty minutes later, we arrive at her parents' house. I turn the car off and take a deep breath, pulling the keys out of the ignition.

I look at Alison and caress her cheek. Her smile is like a sudden beam of sunlight as the corners of her mouth lift upwards, and those icy blue eyes stare into mine. I lean in and kiss her soft lips. "I'm so glad you're safe."

"I love you," her voice is soft, pure, and sweet.

I kiss her lips again and open my car door to get out. I look around at my surroundings. A lot of green, a lot of trees. It's dreadful. Woods aren't fun to look at after what I just went through. Alison holds onto my arm. She has been clinging to me since I got her out of that hellhole.

I place the key into the doorknob, turn it, and push the door in.

"Alison, oh my god, baby girl!" Her mom comes in and reaches out her arms for a hug.

"Mom, please fill me in on everything from the beginning," Alison says, letting go of the hug.

"Honey, there's so much to go over," Kayla says, taking Alison's hand and leading us into the living room to sit.

I sit next to Alison on the brown leather couch and look at Kayla.

"Alex and I are not on speaking terms, if that is what you are concerned about," I say.

She shakes her head, lifts a binder off the table, and places it in her lap.

"This binder explains things you may find hard to believe." She opens it and flips through a few sheets of paper, sighing before handing it to us.

The pages show images of a man and woman lying in a hospital bed. I take a closer look, and the faces seem a little too familiar.

The woman is Alison. I look at her and look at the image.

"This is Alison? It can't be. The year shows 1922."

"What?" She takes the binder from my grip and looks at it.

"The man is you, Jason," Alison says.

I take the binder back and look at the man, and sure enough, it's me.

"Wait, there's a photo of another man!" Alison says.

I look at the photo she's pointing at and widen my eyes.

"That's officer Kevin Dawson," I say.

"Who?" Alison asks.

"He was the one who wouldn't help me look for you. I fucking knew he was involved!" I slam the binder on the coffee table in front of me.

"Why is he in this photo?" I ask, looking straight at my mother-in-law.

"It's because he was involved the same way you two are."

"What does this mean, Mom?" Alison asks.

Kayla sighs and clasps her hands together before placing them on her lap. "Your adventure isn't quite finished just yet. If you went into the past and did something, you could see what they did as those events have already occurred. They are you, but not quite. Copies, per se."

"So, what you're saying is we can go back and find out more about this entire situation?" I ask.

"Yes. And your mission will be to stop them."

LET'S CONNECT

Amy Rose

hello@amyjudithrose.com

Website: amyjudithrose.com

Social Media:

TikTok: amyroseauthor

Instagram: @amyjudithrose

ABOUT THE AUTHOR

Amy Rose was born and raised in Springfield, Illinois.

She has a deep love for romance, fantasy, dystopian, and action/adventure book genres. Although, her absolute favorite is fantasy.

Amy's writing journey began in the second grade when her teacher gave her a personal journal. Since then, writing has been a huge passion and something she will never stop doing.

Over the years, she faced many mental and physical struggles from ADHD, Asperger's, Depression, Panic Disorder, and Chronic Pain, but she has never allowed the challenges to stop her nor define who she is.